FOR HENRY

Anne Wilsdorf

PRINCESS

Based on Hans Christian Andersen's
"The Princess and the Pea"

Greenwillow Books, New York

Library of Congress Cataloging-in-Publication Data
Wilsdorf, Anne.
[Princesse. English]
Princess : based on Hans Christian Andersen's "The princess
and the pea" / by Anne Wilsdorf.
p.   cm.
Translation of: Princesse.
Summary: A girl proves that she is a real princess in an unusual way.
ISBN 0-688-11541-1 (trade). ISBN 0-688-11542-X (lib. bdg.)
[1. Fairy tales.]   I. Andersen, H. C. (Hans Christian), 1805–1875.
Prindsessen paa aerten.   II. Title.   PZ8.W6815Pr   1993
[E]—dc20   92-20636   CIP   AC

Leopold was a prince who lived in a castle with his mother, the queen, and his father, the king. He dreamed of adventure, travel, and love.

"Farewell, dear mother," he said. "I am off to find the princess of my dreams."

"Farewell, then," said the queen. "But remember, Leopold, no one but a genuine princess can have the honor of marrying my son."

She handed him a list of certified genuine princesses and said, "Be careful. Each of them is guarded by an evil monster who must be vanquished before the princess will be free to marry."

Then she kissed him and sent him on his way.

The first princess on the list was Marisa Ping.
Full of ardor, the prince made his way to her castle.
He was greeted by a horrible videopteryx, spitting
fire and flames.

"This should be easy," said Leopold.
ZIP! He unsheathed his sword. ZAP! Off came
the monster's head.

"Marisa Ping, will you marry me?" asked Leopold.
But the princess was too busy watching television to answer.
I wonder what I would have done if she had said yes, thought
Leopold. This princess is not for me.

He continued on to the next castle on the list.
It was guarded by a ferocious antiseptyx.

Leopold stunned the antiseptyx with one blow
and went into the castle.

The princess appeared, waving a dishcloth and duster.
"Don't step on my clean floor with your dirty feet!" she
said crossly. "Here is a pair of slippers to put on over
your shoes."
"No, thank you," said the prince, and he turned his
horse around. "Not my type at all," he said sadly.

At the castle of the third princess, a threatening bombachyderm blocked the way. Leopold chopped it into slices.

"Bravo! Long live my warrior! Long live violence! Long live everything horrible! Kill 'em dead!" shouted the princess.

"Oh dear, she's too bloodthirsty for me," said Leopold with a sigh, and he rode away.

The castle of Jubelle, the fourth princess on the list,
was nearby, so the prince decided to try again. But a three-
headed narcissyx wouldn't let him past the gate.
"This is getting tedious," said the prince as he prepared to fight.

WHAM! In no time the terrifying beast
was all tied up.

While all this was going on, Jubelle was staring into her mirror, saying over and over, "Oh, but I am beautiful. How beautiful I am. I can't get over my own beauty." "This beauty is not for me," said Leopold. "I don't like any of these princesses. I guess I will have to go home without a wife."

On his way back it started to rain.
Leopold took cover in a shed.

He was not alone.
"How do you do?" he said.
"I am Prince Leopold."

"My father calls me Princess," said the stranger.
"I am a shepherdess. I have been traveling through the land,
  looking for a nice shepherd to marry. I haven't found him,
  so I am going back to my parents and my sheep."

The prince told her about his own adventures, and they
discovered that they had a lot in common. They looked at
each other in wonder.
"You are exactly the one I have been looking for!" each said
to the other.
And the prince put Princess on his horse and started home.

"Mother," said Prince Leopold, "I would like you to meet Princess."

The queen looked at the girl. "A princess?" she said to herself. "That raggedy girl? I'll soon find out if she is a genuine princess. I'll put her to the pea test. If she is really a princess, she shall marry my son. If she is not, that will be the end of her."

The queen took the smallest pea she could find. She put it at the bottom of a tall stack of feather mattresses in Princess's bedroom. Only the skin of a genuine princess would be delicate enough to feel the pea and be bruised by it.

Princess climbed up the ladder and into the bed.

But during the night, forgetting how high she was, she started
to get up for a drink of water—and fell all the way to the floor.
She was bruised and miserable and had a hard time falling asleep again.

In the morning the queen came running into
the bedroom. She saw at once that Princess
had not slept well.

And when the girl got out of bed, the queen
saw black-and-blue bruises all over her body.
"Princess!" she cried.

And the wedding was arranged at once.

Princess and Leopold set out to live happily ever after....

"He's a nice boy," Princess's parents agreed later.
"But where did she find herself a shepherd
who knows so little about sheep?"

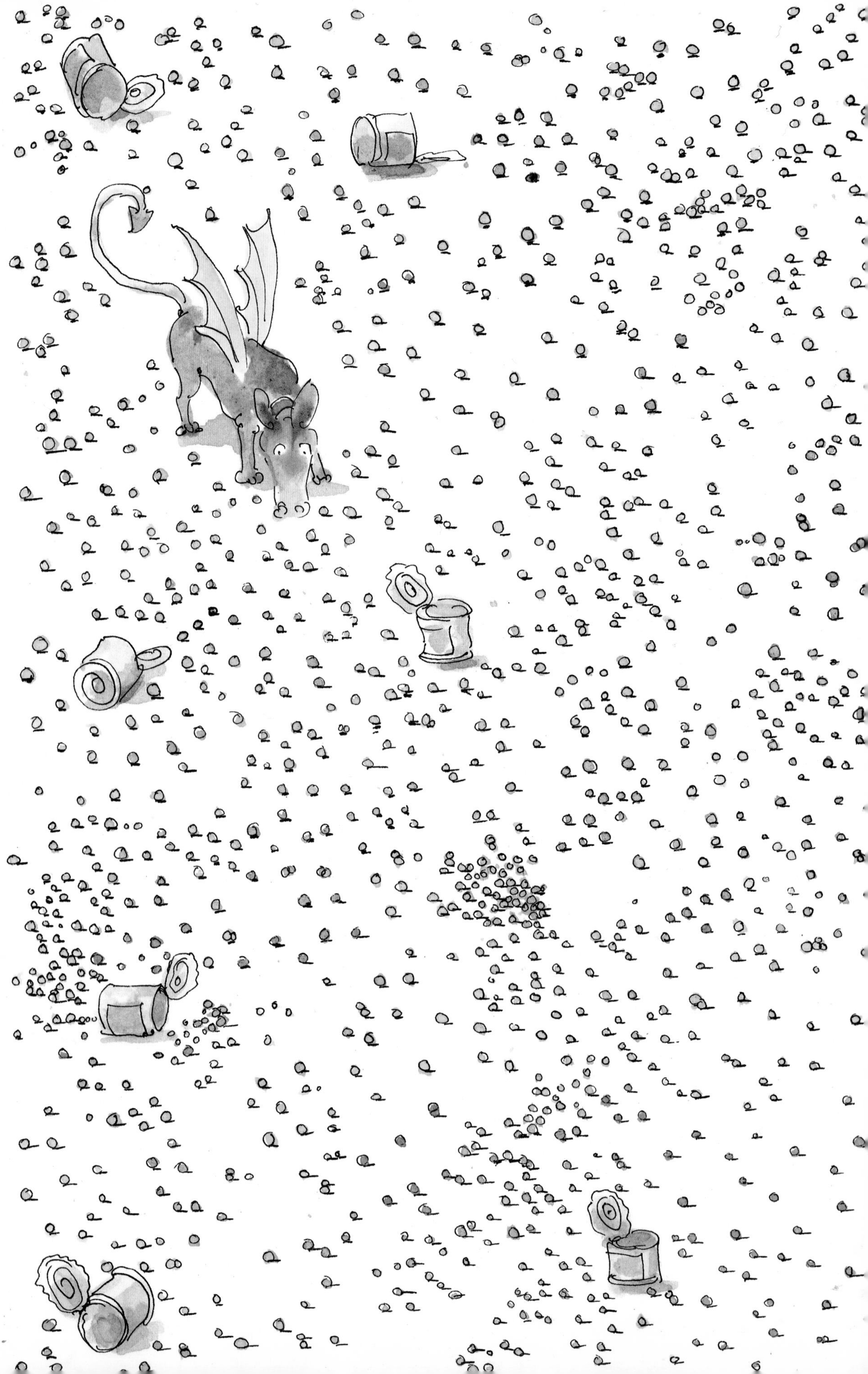